W9-BER-432

In the name of Allah, the One God, the Most Compassionate, the Most Merciful

Cinderella
AN ISLAMIC TALE

Retold by
FAWZIA GILANI

Illustrated by
SHIREEN ADAMS

Once upon a time there lived a rich and noble man and a kind and beautiful lady.

They had a daughter named Zahra who was sweet and gentle, and as beautiful as the crescent moon. Every day Zahra and her parents would read the Qur'an, and they never missed a prayer.

As the months passed by Zahra's mother became ill. Although many doctors had been called, no one could find a cure. One sad day Zahra's mother died. Father and daughter were heartbroken.

'*Inna lillahi wa inna ilayhi raji'un,*' said the father with tears in his eyes. 'Truly, we belong to Allah and to Him we will return.'
Zahra and her father were very sad, but they put their trust in Allah and asked Him to grant them patience and comfort.

After some time the father decided to marry again. He married a widow with two daughters. In the beginning, the new wife tried to be loving and caring. But as time went on she saw how graceful Zahra was compared to her own daughters. This made her extremely jealous. She saw that while Zahra was beautiful and elegant, her own daughters were plain and clumsy. While Zahra was humble and giving, her own daughters were proud and selfish. And while Zahra was gentle and kind, the stepmother's daughters were rough and cruel.

This was more than the stepmother could bear, and darkness grew in her heart. When her husband was away, the stepmother was harsh and unfair to the girl. She made Zahra do most of the housework while her own lazy daughters slept or played. But Zahra was forgiving and patient, and never complained to her father.

A few years later, Zahra's father became very ill. One day he called his daughter to his side and gave her words of love and advice.

'My sweet child,' he said, 'Follow the Qur'an and the Sunnah, and never miss your prayers. Be patient and humble, always speak gently and share whatever you have with the poor. And know that I love you very much. May Allah protect you and make you a strong Muslim.'

The poor child clung to her father.

'You must hold fast to the rope of Allah and never let go,' he said.

'*La ilaha ill-Allah Muhammadur rasulullah*.' These were the last words her father spoke.

'*Inna lillahi wa inna ilayhi raji'un*,' whispered the poor girl as she wept. Zahra was alone in the world. She was an orphan with no one to love her.

After her father died, the stepmother took away Zahra's beautiful clothes and gave her old clothes and rags to wear. Then she took away her bedroom and made her sleep in the attic. From that time on Zahra was ordered to do all the housework.

One day, as the poor orphan was tending the fireplace, some live cinders fell on her dress and burned holes into it. Trying to put out the cinders, she became covered with soot. Her stepsisters began to laugh at her. 'Cinder-ella! Cinder-ella!' they teased and taunted. After that they no longer used her real name, but only called her 'Cinderella'.

The orphaned child felt very sad. She missed her mother and father very much. She often thought of them. When she prayed, she would make special *du'as* in *sujud*.

"*Du'as* made in *sujud* reach Allah swiftly," her mother had told her.

"Be patient, my child," her father had encouraged.

Cinderella was always patient. She read the Qur'an every day and comforted herself with the words of God and stories of God's Messengers.

Cinderella would wake early at *fajr* before sunrise and do her morning prayers. Then she would sit and read the Qur'an. When she had finished she would prepare breakfast for her stepmother and stepsisters. Then the poor orphan would wash the dishes, wipe the counters, make the beds, sweep and mop the floors. At noon she would offer her midday prayers and quickly eat her lunch.

When Cinderella felt lonely she would take the crumbs she had saved from the table and feed the birds. She would watch them chirp and peck as she washed the dishes.

When her kitchen work was done she would sometimes join them, quietly singing a song of her own. Cinderella spent her whole day working. When she was not cooking, washing, ironing or dusting she would find a little time to read her books in her tiny, little attic, sitting on her old, thin mattress.

Cinderella always served dinner to her stepmother and stepsisters in the dining room. She was never invited to join them; instead she was told to sit alone in the kitchen and eat the leftovers. By the time she had offered her nighttime prayers, she was very tired. She would recite some *surahs* before she closed her eyes and then whisper the *shahadah*. The more difficulties Cinderella faced, the stronger her *iman* grew. Meanwhile, her stepmother and stepsisters became lazier and more arrogant each day.

One day an invitation arrived from the King's palace. A huge party was to be held on the evening of the first day of *Eid al-Adha*, the celebration after Hajj. The stepsisters were all aflutter about what they should wear. Cinderella was just as excited; the thought of going to the palace and attending an Eid party sounded wonderful.

'Could I please wear one of your dresses?' Cinderella asked shyly, while her stepsisters
eagerly looked through their closets. They swung round and looked at her with disgust.
'Wear one of our dresses?!' shouted the stepsisters together. 'Never!'
'How dare you even think of going to the palace!' scolded the younger stepsister.
'You belong in the cinders, not in a palace!' yelled the older stepsister.
'Yes, Cinderella,' said the stepmother peering down at the orphan, 'there will be very
important people at the palace. It's not a place for someone like you.'
Both stepsisters screeched with laughter and returned to their closets to choose a dress.

Cinderella looked at her torn, old dress and thought of a Qur'anic verse she had read,

Truly the most honoured of you in Allah's eyes is the one who is most righteous.[1]

Then she reminded herself of the words of the beloved Prophet,⋆

'Truly, Allah does not look at your faces and your wealth, but He looks at your hearts and your deeds.'[2]

Later that evening, Cinderella opened her hadith book and read,

The Prophet Muhammad⋆ said: 'Fasting on the Day of 'Arafah removes the sins of two years: the past and the coming year.'[3]

'*Alhamdulillah!*' said Cinderella, 'Tomorrow is the Day of '*Arafah*. I will fast tomorrow, *inshallah*.' And with that intention she fell asleep. During the night Cinderella dreamt of her grandmother, who years ago had left to make Hajj. She had never returned and most people believed she had died during the journey.

Late that night, before the sky's first light, Cinderella heard the call of a cockerel and awoke suddenly. She smiled, thankful that she had woken in time to eat *sahoor*. She crept down to the kitchen and quickly ate and drank her meal. Then, during that blessed part of the night when Zahra knew that Allah listens to special requests, she prayed two *rak'ahs* and made a *du'a*.

'Dear Allah, I would really like to go to the palace for the Eid party. If it is good for my faith, and for my life in this world and the Next, please let me go. *Ameen*.'

The sun arose and brought the beautiful day of *Eid al-Adha*. Cinderella was very excited. She washed, dressed and made herself ready to go to the Eid prayer.

'And where do you think you're going?' snapped the stepmother.

'Oh, it's Eid. With your permission, I would like to attend the Eid prayers,' said Cinderella.

'You will not go to the Eid prayer!' hissed the stepmother, 'You will help my daughters get ready for the Eid party!'

Tears filled Cinderella's eyes, but she looked down to the floor and thought of another Qur'anic verse she had memorised:

Allah does not place on any soul a burden greater than it can bear...

(So) pray... 'O Lord, do not lay a greater burden on us than we have the strength to bear!

Remove our sins, forgive us, and have mercy on us!

You are our Protector; so help us against those who stand against faith.[4]

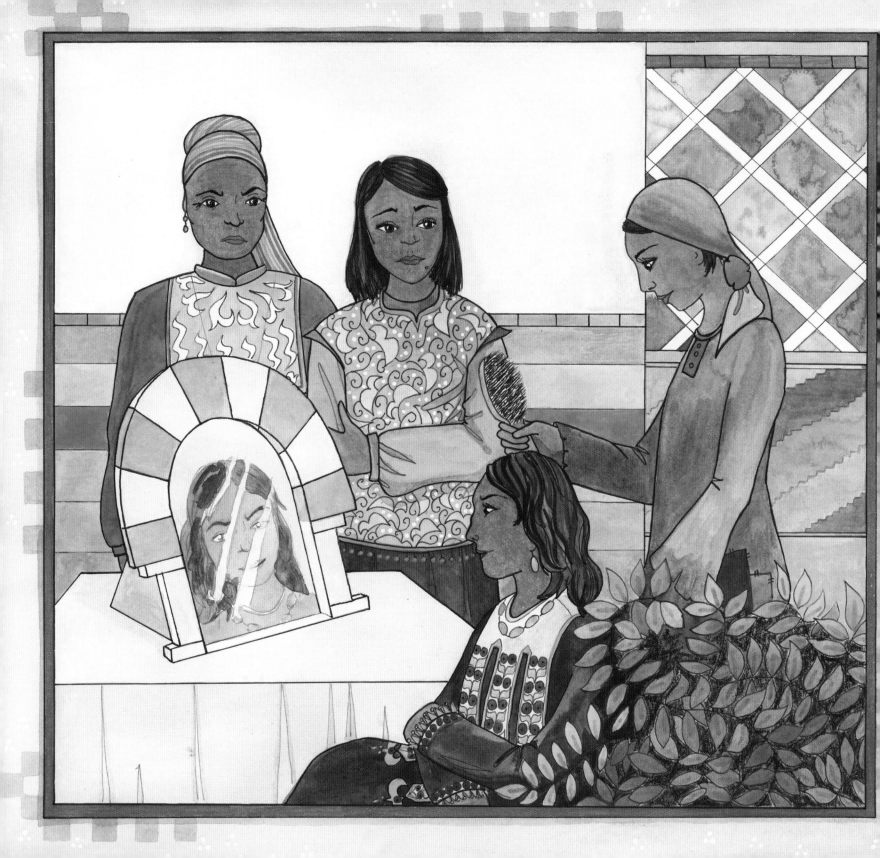

All day long Cinderella helped her stepsisters prepare for the Eid party. She ironed their dresses, polished their shoes, and went to the jeweller to mend a necklace. When she returned, she began to work on their hair and makeup.
At last it was time for the stepsisters and stepmother to leave.

'Dear stepmother,' Cinderella asked once again, 'may I please attend the Eid party?'
At first the stepmother's face flushed red with anger, but then she said, 'Very well, Cinderella, you may come to the party after you have finished *all* your chores.'
'But stepmother, I'll miss the party if I don't leave now,' said Cinderella.
'Once you've finished *all* your chores,' repeated the stepmother coldly, 'and only then!'

Cinderella stood at the door and watched them go. She felt very lonely and very, very sad. She thought of a Qur'anic verse,

For those who are patient and do good deeds, there is forgiveness and a great reward.[5]

Cinderella went inside with a lump in her throat and began to pick up the dresses that lay scattered around the room. Suddenly there was a loud knock at the door.

Cinderella walked to the door and peered through the peephole. Seeing an old woman in *hijab*, she opened it.

'*As-salamu alaykum,*' said Cinderella, curiously.

'*Wa alaykum as-salam,* my child!' said the old woman, warmly. Beyond the step, Cinderella saw a grand coach with beautiful horses and six attendants, dressed in magnificent costumes.

'*Mashallah,*' said Cinderella looking at the splendid sight, 'you must have come for my stepmother and stepsisters. I'm sorry, but they have already left.'

'No,' said the old woman, whose face looked vaguely familiar, 'I did not come for them.' The old lady paused and then continued. 'My dear child, I came for you.' Cinderella stared at the old lady and then sadly shook her head. 'You are very kind," she stammered, holding back her tears, "*Jazaki Allahu khayran.* I'm so sorry but I can't go. I don't have party clothes and…' she sighed, 'I don't have time. I have to finish my chores.' Cinderella glanced around at the mess.

'But please,' said Cinderella as she looked up into the kind eyes of the stranger, 'May I ask who I have the honour of addressing?'

'Sweet Zahra, you did not recognize me,' said the old woman. 'It is true that you haven't seen me for many years, but as I look at you, I see your dear mother's face in your own.'

Cinderella stared into the stranger's gentle eyes. Then she flung her arms around the old woman.

'Grandmother!' she sobbed. 'I saw you in my dream! Where have you been?'

The old woman held Cinderella in her arms for a long time.

'Dear child,' said Cinderella's grandmother, 'On my return from Hajj, I passed through a country that was at war. For many years the people were not free to travel. But we will speak of these things another time. *Alhamdulillah,* I am back now. Come,' she said, 'let us go.'

'But I still have to clean the house,' said Cinderella.

Grandmother clapped her hands, and the six attendants entered the house and began to clean.

'Dear Grandmother, what about my clothes?' asked Cinderella. Grandmother clapped her hands again. Three ladies appeared with a dress, a green *abaya*, a headscarf, and two glass slippers. Quickly, Cinderella washed and made wudu, and then the ladies arranged her hair and scarf, and helped her with her clothing. Finally, they gently slid delicate glass slippers onto her feet.

Cinderella looked in a mirror. She looked elegant and very happy. She took her grandmother's arm and sat in the beautiful coach. In no time at all, they reached the palace.

'Now remember, my dear,' cautioned the grandmother, as they arrived at the palace, 'the party will end soon after 11 o'clock. You must return home by then– before your stepmother and stepsisters. I will be waiting for you in the coach.' '*Inshallah*, dear Grandmother, I will,' promised Cinderella, as she kissed her goodbye and said her salaam.

Cinderella walked in through the ladies' entrance, passing her stepsisters. She greeted and smiled at them as she walked by.
The stepsisters just stared at Cinderella, wondering who she was.
'She's very pretty,' whispered the older girl.
'Everyone is looking at her,' said the younger one.
All the ladies and girls watched Cinderella. They wondered who the lovely, radiant young woman was, dressed in full *hijab*. Other beautiful girls were there, too, but only Cinderella walked with a graceful modesty and inner light that comes from a life of *taqwa*.

Cinderella caught the attention of the King, the Queen and Prince Bilal
as they passed her in the large hallway.
'Who is that girl in the green *abaya* and headscarf?' asked the Prince.
Nobody seemed to know.

The Queen came to greet Cinderella in the ladies' hall, and asked
Cinderella to sit beside her while the *Eid* program was presented.
The drummers drummed, the singers sang, the acrobats performed.
Delicious trays of food were served. Then the *adhan* was called.
Most of the women continued to talk through the *adhan* but
Cinderella remained silent.

When the prayer began, most of the women continued to eat, but
Cinderella joined those who went to pray. She impressed the Queen
with her graceful speech and behaviour. Cinderella was so happy.
The poor girl could not remember having such a wonderful time.

Suddenly, Cinderella noticed people preparing to leave. It was eleven o'clock! Mumbling an excuse, Cinderella quickly left the hall. As she rushed into the coach to join her grandmother, her glass slipper slid off her foot and fell to the ground. Just at that moment, her stepmother came out of the palace door.

'Please hurry!' said Cinderella to the coachman, 'I must get home!' and she left her slipper behind. Meanwhile, the prince walked down the palace steps and picked up the delicate glass slipper.

The prince returned to the Queen holding the glass slipper.
'Mother,' said Prince Bilal, 'I saw many young ladies today. But I saw no one with more *taqwa* and beauty than the girl in the green *hijab*. That is the girl I wish to marry.'

The Queen smiled. '*Subhanallah*,' she said, 'It is rare to find young ladies with such good character. *Inshallah* you will marry the girl who has *iman*, the girl to whom this glass slipper belongs.' The Queen sighed and then continued, 'But first we must find her – she disappeared before I could ask who she was!'

'Now, my child,' said Grandmother, as she helped Cinderella out of the coach, 'When your stepmother arrives you must not let her know I was here. *Inshallah* I will return for you tomorrow– I promise.'

She hurriedly kissed and hugged Cinderella and gave her *salam*. The grand-mother quickly left with her attendants. Cinderella hid her Eid dress in the attic and put the remaining glass slipper carefully into a wooden chest under her bed. No sooner had she done so when her stepmother and stepsisters returned.

'Oh, we met such a beautiful girl at the palace!' said the stepsisters to Cinderella. 'She fussed over us and kept wanting to talk with us,' lied the older stepsister, looking vainly at herself in the mirror.
'Yes, she took our hand and even wanted us to sit beside the Queen,' added the younger stepsister, adding another lie.
'*Mashallah*,' said Cinderella. 'I'm glad you had such a wonderful time.'

The next morning the whole town was buzzing with excitement. The King and Queen had announced that their son wished to marry the girl whose foot fitted into the glass slipper he had found. The Queen's lady-in-waiting was to go to each home that had received an invitation, and allow the young ladies of the house to try on the glass slipper.

'I'm sure the slipper will fit me,' said the younger stepsister.

'My foot is smaller,' said the older sister, 'it will fit me.'

The stepsisters began to argue, when suddenly there was a loud knock on the door.

Cinderella went to see who it was.

'*As-salamu 'alaykum*,' said Cinderella as she opened the door.

'*Wa 'alaykum as-salam*,' replied the Queen's lady-in-waiting. She held a chest containing the delicate glass slipper. Cinderella excused herself and hurried to the attic, and took her glass slipper out of the wooden chest. She hid it in her apron pocket.

Meanwhile the older stepsister was the first to try on the slipper. But no matter how hard she tried, her foot was far too big. Then the second stepsister tried on the slipper, but her toes were far too wide.

The Queen's lady then looked around and saw Cinderella coming down the stairs.

'You must also try on the glass slipper,' she said.

'That's absurd!' said the younger stepsister, 'Cinderella is just a housecleaner!'

'She's a maid!' blurted the older stepsister.

'Nevertheless,' said the Queen's lady, 'all the young women of the house have been ordered to try on the glass slipper.' She stepped forward and gave Cinderella the slipper. Cinderella took the slipper and placed it on her foot. To the complete amazement of the stepsisters and stepmother, it fitted!

Then Cinderella reached into her pocket and pulled out the other glass slipper and slid it onto her other foot. The stepsisters stood with their mouths wide open. They could hardly believe that Cinderella was the same girl they had so admired at the party.

The stepmother grew red with anger and envy.

'You!' she shouted. 'You do not have my permission to marry!'

Just then, the doors swung open and Grandmother walked in.

'My grandchild may not have your permission to marry,' said the old woman firmly, 'but, *alhamdulillah*, she has mine!'

The stepmother and stepsisters could only stare in astonishment.

And so it was agreed. Prince Bilal was very happy to hear that his bride had been found, and so was Cinderella. They were married in a joyous ceremony and from that day on, the lovely Zahra was never called Cinderella again.

Princess Zahra lived happily ever after with her husband– along with the King, the Queen, and her grandmother, who was given a special house on the palace grounds. Through Princess Zahra's good character and example many people increased their faith and good deeds during her long and happy life.

As for the stepmother and stepsisters, when they saw how Allah had rewarded Zahra's goodness, they were filled with shame. They repented for their sins and asked for her forgiveness. And, remembering the example of the Prophet Yusuf* and his brothers, Princess Zahra forgave them wholeheartedly.

For, as Allah says,
> *Can the reward for goodness be anything but goodness?*[6]

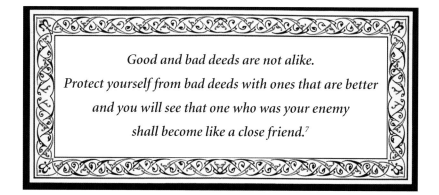

> *Good and bad deeds are not alike.*
> *Protect yourself from bad deeds with ones that are better*
> *and you will see that one who was your enemy*
> *shall become like a close friend.*[7]

Abaya – An overgarment worn by Muslim women and older girls.

Adhan – The call to prayer for one of the five daily prayers.

Alhamdulillah – 'Praise be to God.'

Ameen – 'Amen'; said at the end of a prayer or supplication.

As-salamu 'alaykum; wa 'alaykum as-salam – 'Peace be with you'/'And on you be peace'.

Day of 'Arafah – The day that pilgrims gather on Mount Arafat, at the end of the Hajj.

Du'a – Supplication; personal prayer.

Eid al-Adha – The Feast of the Sacrifice held at the end of the Pilgrimage.

Fajr – Dawn.

Hijab – Headscarf worn by practising Muslim women and girls.

Iman – Faith.

Inna lillahi wa inna ilayhi raji'un – 'From God we come and to Him do we return'.

Inshallah – God-willing.

Jazaki Allahu khayran – 'May God reward your goodness' (feminine grammatical form).

La ilaha ill-Allah, Muhammadur-Rasulullah – 'There is no god but Allah (the One God), and Muhammad is the Messenger of God.' The Islamic declaration of faith.

Mashallah – 'God has willed it'; said when admiring something or someone.

Rak'ah – A unit or cycle of the ritual prayer.

Sahoor – Late night breakfast taken during Ramadan before the first light of dawn.

Shahadah – The Islamic declaration of faith (see 'La ilaha ill-Allah', above).

Subhanallah – 'Glory be to God.'

Sujud – Prostration with one's head on the ground, as performed during the ritual prayer.

Surah – Chapter of the holy Qur'an.

Taqwa – Piety; God-consciousness.